Marx
Defoe Abbott Hardy Montaigne Machiavelli Chesterton Cooper Emerson Joyce Austen
Melville Haggard Hugo Grimm Eliot
Stoker Christie Molière
Wilde Carroll Maupassant Byron Schiller
Garnett Einstein Fitzgerald Engels
Goethe Hawthorne Smith Kafka Hall
Cotton Dostoyevsky
Baum Henry Kipling Doyle Willis
Leslie Dumas Flaubert Nietzsche
Stockton Turgenev Balzac
Burroughs Vatsyayana Crane
Curtis Tocqueville Verne
Homer Widger Whitman Gogol Vinci
Darwin Tolstoy Busch
Potter Freud Thoreau Twain Scott
Kant Zola Lawrence Plato Harte
Jowett Stevenson Dickens Hesse
Andersen Burton
London Descartes Cervantes
Poe Aristotle Wells Voltaire Cooke
Hale James Hastings
Bunner Shakespeare Irving
Richter Chambers
Doré Dante Chekhov da Shaw Wodehouse Benedict Alcott
Swift Pushkin
Newton

 tredition®

tredition was established in 2006 by Sandra Latusseck and Soenke Schulz. Based in Hamburg, Germany, tredition offers publishing solutions to authors and publishing houses, combined with world-wide distribution of printed and digital book content. tredition is uniquely positioned to enable authors and publishing houses to create books on their own terms and without conventional manu-facturing risks.

For more information please visit: www.tredition.com

TREDITION CLASSICS

This book is part of the TREDITION CLASSICS series. The creators of this series are united by passion for literature and driven by the intention of making all public domain books available in printed format again - worldwide. Most TREDITION CLASSICS titles have been out of print and off the bookstore shelves for decades. At tredition we believe that a great book never goes out of style and that its value is eternal. Several mostly non-profit literature projects provide content to tredition. To support their good work, tredition donates a portion of the proceeds from each sold copy. As a reader of a TREDITION CLASSICS book, you support our mission to save many of the amazing works of world literature from oblivion. See all available books at www.tredition.com.

Project Gutenberg

The content for this book has been graciously provided by Project Gutenberg. Project Gutenberg is a non-profit organization founded by Michael Hart in 1971 at the University of Illinois. The mission of Project Gutenberg is simple: To encourage the creation and distribution of eBooks. Project Gutenberg is the first and largest collection of public domain eBooks.

The Busted Ex-Texan and Other Stories

W. H. H. (William Henry Harrison) Murray

Imprint

THE BUSTED EX-TEXAN AND OTHER STORIES

BY

W. H. H. MUR-

RAY

W.H.H. Murray

THE

BUSTED EX-TEXAN

AND

OTHER STORIES

BY

W. H. H. MURRAY

AUTHOR OF "DAYLIGHT LAND," "THE STORY THE KEG TOLD ME,"
"ADIRONDACK ADVENTURES," ETC.

PHOTOGRAVURE PORTRAIT AND EIGHT FULL-PAGE ILLUS-
TRATIONS
BY THOS. WORTH.

BOSTON
DE WOLFE, FISKE & CO., PUBLISHERS

1890

ILLUSTRATIONS.

THE BUSTED EX-TEXAN.

WE were camped amid the foot-hills on the trail which led up to the Kicking Horse Pass. The sun had already passed from sight, beyond the white summits above us, and the shadow of the monstrous mountain range darkened the prairie to the east, to the horizon's rim. Our bivouac was made in a grove of lofty firs, six or eight in number; and a little rivulet, trickling from the upper slopes, fell, with soft, lapsing sound, within a few feet of our camp-fire. We did not even pitch a tent, for the sky was mild, and above us the monstrous trees lifted their protecting canopy of stems. The hammocks were swung for the ladies, and each gentleman "preëmpted" the claim that suited him best, by depositing his [Pg 6] blanket and rifle upon it. The entire party were in the best of spirits, and nature responded to our happiness in its kindest mood. Laughter sounded pleasantly at intervals from the busy groups, each working at some self-appointed industry. The hum of cheerful conversation mingled with the murmurs of the brook; and now and then the snatch of some sweet song would break from tuneful lips, brief, spirited, melodious as a bobolink's, dashing upward from the clover-heads. And before the mighty shadow lying gloomily on the great prairie plain, which stretched eastward for a thousand miles, had grown to darkness, the active, happy workers had given to the bivouac that look of designed orderliness which a trained party always give to any spot they select in which to make a camp or pass a night. An hour before, there was nothing to distinguish that grove of trees, or the ground beneath them, from any other spot or hill within the reach of eye. But now it commanded the [Pg 7] landscape; and, had you been trailing over the vast plain, the bright firelight, the group of men and women moving to and fro, the picketed horses, the fluttering bits of color here and there, would have caught your gaze ten miles away; and were you tired or hungry, or even lonesome, you would have naturally turned your horse's head toward that camp as toward a cheerful reception and a home; for wherever is happy human life, to it all lonely life is drawn as by a magnet.

And this was demonstrated by our experience then and there. For, scarcely had we done with supper,—and by this time the gloom had grown to darkness, and the half-light of evening held the landscape,—when out of the semi-gloom there came a call,—the call of a man hailing a camp. Indeed, we were not sure he had not hailed several times before we heard him; for, to tell the truth, we were a very merry crowd, and as light of heart as if there was not a worry or care in all the world, [Pg 8] —at least for us,—and the smallest spark of a joke exploded us like a battery. Indeed, so rollicking was our mood that our laughter was nearly continuous, and it is quite possible that the stranger may have hailed us more than once without our hearing him. And this was the more likely because the man's voice was not of the loudest, nor was it positive in the energy of its appeal.

Indeed, there was a certain feebleness or timidity in the stranger's hail, as if he was mistrustful that any good fortune could respond to him, and, hence, deprecated the necessity of the resort. But hear him we did at last, and he was greeted with a chorus of voices to "Come in! Come in! You're welcome!" And partly because we had finished our repast, and partly from courtesy and the natural promptings of gentlefolk to give a visitor courteous greeting, we all arose and received him standing. And, certainly, had the kindly act been unusual with us, not one of our group [Pg 9] would have regretted the extra condescension bestowed upon him at his coming, after he had entered the circle of our firelight, and we saw the expression of his features.

What a mirror the human face is! Looking into it, how we behold the soul, the accidents that have befallen it and the disappointments it has borne! Are not the faces of men as carved tablets on which we read the records of their lives? The face of childhood is smoothly beautiful, like a white page on which neither with ink of red or black has any pen drawn character. But, as the years go on, the pen begins to move and the fatal tracery to grow,—that tracery which means and tells so much. And the face of this man,—this waif, so to speak,—this waif that had come to us from the stretch of the prairie, whose southern line is the southern gulf; this stranger, who had come so suddenly to the circle of our light, and so plaintively sought admission to its comfort and its cheer, was a face which one might read [Pg 10] at a glance. Not one in our circle that did not instantly feel that he embodied some overwhelming calamity. A look of sadness, of a mild, continuous sorrow, overspread his face. There was a pitiful expression about the mouth, as if brave determination had withdrawn its lines from it forever. From his eyes a certain mistrustfulness looked forth,—not mistrustfulness of others, but of himself,—as if confidence in his own powers had received an overwhelming shock. The man's appearance made an instant and unmistakable impression upon the entire company. The ladies—God bless their sweet and sympathetic natures!—were profoundly moved at the pitiful aspect of our guest. Their bosoms thrilled with sympathy for one upon whose devoted head evil fortune had so evidently emptied its quiver. Nor were our less sensitive masculine natures untouched by his forlorn appearance.

"A target for evil fortune," whispered Dick to the major. [Pg 11]

"A regular bull's-eye!" was the solemn response. "A bull's-eye, by gad! at the end of the score."

It was not a poetic expression. I wish the reader to note that I do not record it as such. I only preserve it as evidence of the major's humanity, and of the unaffected sympathy for the stranger, which at that moment filled all hearts.

Naturally, as it can well be imagined, the gayety of our company had been utterly checked by the coming of our sad guest. In the presence of such a wreck of human happiness, perhaps of human hope, what person of any sensibility could maintain a lightsome mood? Had it not been for one peculiarity,—a peculiarity, I am confident, all of us observed,—the depression of our spirits would have been as profound as it was universal. This peculiarity was the stranger's appetite. This, fortunately, had remained unimpaired,—an oasis in the Sahara of his life. [Pg 12]

"The one remnant left him from the wreck of his fortunes," whispered Dick.

"A perfect remnant!" returned the major, sententiously.

For myself, acting as host to this appetite, and being naturally of a philosophic turn, I watched its development with the keenest interest, not to say with a growing curiosity. "Here is something," I said to myself, "that is unique. That fine law of recompense which is kindly distributed through the universe finds here," I reflected, "a most instructive and conclusive demonstration. Robbed, by an adverse fate, of all that made life agreeable, this man, this pilgrim of time, this wayfarer to eternity, this companion of mine on the road of life, has had bestowed upon him an extraordinary solace, has been permitted to retain a commensurate satisfaction. Surely, life cannot have lost its attractions for one whose stomach still preserves such aspirations." And, prompted by the benevolence of my mood, and the antici [Pg 13] pations of a wise forecast, I collected in front of me whatever edibles remained on the table, that, if the supply of our hospitality should prove insufficient, the exhibition of its spirit should at least be conclusive.

But, if the countenance of the stranger was of a most melancholy cast, there were not lacking hints that by nature he had been endowed with vivacity of spirit; for, as he continued, with an industry which was remarkable, to refresh himself, there were appearances, which came to the eye and the corners of his mouth, which made the observer conclude that he was not lacking the sense of humor; and, if his experience had been most unfortunate, there was in him an ability to appreciate the ludicrousness of its changeful situations. Indeed, one could but conclude that originally he must have been of a buoyant, not to say sanguine disposition; and, if one could but prevail upon him to narrate the incidents of his life, they would be found to be most entertaining. [Pg 14]

It was something like an hour before our melancholy-looking guest had fully improved the opportunity with which a benignant Providence had supplied him,—a freak in which, one might conclude, she seldom indulged. He ceased to eat, and sat for a moment gazing pensively at the dishes. It seemed to me—but in this I may possibly be mistaken—that a darker shade of sadness possessed his face at the conclusion than the one that shadowed it so heavily at the beginning of the repast. "The pleasures of hope," I said to myself, "are evidently greater to my species than are those of recollection. Now that there is nothing left for my guest to anticipate, it is evident that memory ceases to excite." And I could but feel that, had our provisions been more abundant, the stranger's appetite would not have been so easily appeased. With something of regret in my voice, I sought to divert his mind from that sense of disappointment which I judged from his countenance threatened to oppress his spirits. [Pg 15]

"Friend," I said, "I doubt not that you have trailed a goodly distance, and your fasting has been long?"

"I have not eaten a meal in two days," was the response.

"Heavens!" exclaimed Dick in an aside to the major. "Is it credible that that man ate two days ago!"

"Gad!" exclaimed the major, "the man's stomach is nothing but a pocket."

"A pocket! I should call it an unexplored cavern!" retorted Dick.

"The direction and reason of your long trail would be interesting," I resumed. "And, if not impertinent, friend, may I ask you whence you have come?"

"I have journeyed from Texas," replied the man, and his voice nearly broke as he said it.

"*Oh!*" exclaimed the ladies, and they sympathetically grouped themselves, anticipating, with true feminine sensitiveness, some terrible dénouement. [Pg 16]

"*Texas!*" I ejaculated.

"*Gad!*" said the major.

"The *Devil!*" said Dick.

"Yes, *Texas!*" repeated the man, and he groaned.

By this time, as any intelligent reader will easily divine, our whole group was in a condition of mild excitement. Several of us had resided in Texas, and we felt that we stood at the threshold of a history,—a history with infinite possibilities in it. For myself, I knew not how to proceed. My position as a host forbade me to interrogate. The sorrows of life are sacred, and my sensitiveness withheld me from thrusting myself within the enclosure of my guest's recollections. That his experiences, could we but be favored with a narration of them, would be entertaining,—painfully entertaining,—I keenly realized; but how to proceed I saw not. I remained silent.

"Yes,"—it was the stranger who broke the silence,—"I am a busted ex-Texan!"

[Pg 17]

I

am a Busted ex-Texan.

The relief that came to me at the instant was indescribable. The path was made plain. We all felt that we were not only on the threshold of a history, but of a narration of that history. The ladies fluttered into position for listening. I could but see it, and so I am bound to record that I saw Dick irreverently punch the major. It was a punch which carried with it the significance of an exclamation. The major received it with the face of a Spartan, but with the grunt of a Chinook chief.

"Friend," I said, "we are accustomed to beguile the evening hours with entertaining descriptions of travels, often of personal incidents of the haps and hazards of life; and, if it would not be disagreeable to you, we would be vastly entertained, beyond doubt, by any narration with which you might favor us of your Texan experiences and of the fortunes which befell you there."

For a few moments, the silence remained unbroken, save by the crackle of the fire and [Pg 18] the soft movement in the great firs overhead, — a movement which is to sound what dawn is to the day; not so much a sound as a feathery suggestion that sound might come. It was a genial hour, and the mood of the hour began to be felt in our own. The warmth of it evidently penetrated the bosom of our guest. He had eaten. He was filled, — appreciably so at least, and that happy feeling, that comfortable sense of fulness, which characterizes the after-dinner hour, pervaded him with its genial glow. He loosened his belt, — another tremendous nudge from Dick, — and a look of contentment softened his features. Whatever storm had wrecked his life, he had now passed beyond its billows, and from the sure haven into which he had been blown he could gaze with complacent resignation, if not with happiness, at the dangers through which he had passed. I am sure that we were all delighted at the brightening appearance of our guest, and felt that, if the story he was to tell us was one which included [Pg 19] disasters, it would at least be lightened by traces of humor and the calm acceptance of a philosophic mind.

"I was born in the State of Connecticut," so our guest began his narration. "I came from a venturesome stock, and the instinct of commercial enterprise may be regarded as hereditary in my family. My grandfather was the first one to discover the tropical attributes

of the beech-wood tree. He first perceived that it contained within
its fibres the pungency of the nutmeg. With a celerity which we
remember with pride in our family, he availed himself of the commercial value of his discovery, and for years did a prosperous trade
on the credulity of mankind. He was a man of humor,—a sense
which has been to some extent transmitted to myself,—he was a
man of humor, and I have no doubt he enjoyed the joke he was
practising on people, fully as much as the profits which the practical
embodiment of his humor brought to his pocket. My father [Pg 20]
was a deacon, a man of true piety and eminently respectable. He
was engaged in the retail-grocery business,—a business which offers opportunities to a person of wit and of an inventive turn of
mind. The butter that he sold was salted invariably by one rule—a
rule which he discovered and applied in the cellar of the store himself; and the sugar which he sold, if it was sanded, was always
sanded by a method which improved rather than detracted from its
appearance."

Here our guest paused a moment, as if enjoying the recollections
of the virtues of his ancestors. His face was as sober as ever, but his
look was one of contentment; and I could but note the suggestion of
merriment—the merriment of a happy memory—in his eye. How
happy it is for an offspring to be able to recall the character of his
forefathers with such liveliness of mind!

"The motive which impelled me towards Texas," he resumed,
"was one which was [Pg 21] natural for me to feel, thus ancestrally
connected. I had heired my father's business,—the deacon, who had
died full of honors, ripe in years, and in perfect peace. But the business did not prosper in my hands; perhaps, I had not heired, with
the business, the deacon's ability,—that accuracy of eye, that gravity
of appearance, that deftness of touch, so to speak, which underlay
his success. Be that as it may, the business did not pay, and without
hesitation I sold it; and, with a comfortable sum for investment, I
journeyed to Texas.

"It is proper for me to remark that the welcome I received was
most cordial. I chose a populous centre for a temporary residence,
and proceeded to look around me. I found the Texans to be a warm-
hearted people, much given to hospitality, and willing, with a

charming disinterestedness, to admit all new-comers, with capital, to the enormous profits of their various enterprises.

"For the first time in my life, I found myself [Pg 22] among a people who were successful in everything they undertook. Their profits were simply enormous. No speculation could possibly fail. However I invested my money, I was assured that I would speedily become a millionnaire. Cotton was a certain crop. Corn was never known to fail. The Texan tobacco was rapidly driving the Cuban out of the market. The aboriginal grapes of the State, of which there were millions of acres waiting for the presses, yielded, as Europe confessed, a wine superior to Champagne. If I preferred herding, all I had to do was to purchase a few sheep and simply sit down. There was no section of the globe where sheep were so prolific, fleeces so thick, or the demands of market so clamorous. And, as for horses, I was assured that no one in Texas who knew the facts of the case would spend any time in raising them. The prairies were full of them, hundreds of thousands of them, all blooded stock, 'true descendants, sir, from the Moorish Barb, distributed [Pg 23] through the whole country at the Spanish invasion.' I need do nothing but purchase fifty thousand acres, fence the territory in, and the enclosed herds would continue to propagate indefinitely. Such were the delightful pictures which my entertainers presented to me. Captivated by the charming manners of my hosts, my sanguine temperament kindled into heat at the touch of their enthusiasm. Where every venture was sure of successful issue, there was no need for deliberation or selection. I invested indiscriminately in all, and waited buoyantly for the results."

Here the stranger paused, compelled, perhaps, by a slight interruption. Dick had retired, closely followed by the major. Our guest certainly was not devoid of humor, and I was convinced, as I watched the play of his features, that he apprehended and appreciated the reason for their retirement. He lifted a plate from the table, inspected it closely, turned it over, gazed contemplatively at its reversed side, and, pois [Pg 24] ing it deftly upon the point of three fingers, quietly remarked:—

"The gentlemen, I judge, have been in Texas?"

"They have," I replied: "we three were there together."

"Ah!"

It was all he said. I might add, it was all that could be said.

At this point, Dick and the major rejoined us. Their eyes showed traces of recent tears. They were still wiping their faces with their handkerchiefs. With that refinement which is characteristic of true gentlemen, and which seeks concealment of any extraordinary emotion, they had considerately retired to indulge their laughter.

"I am delighted," continued our guest, after Dick and the major had resumed their seats, "I am delighted to find myself in company with men of experience. I feel that you will not question the veracity of my story, or fail to [Pg 25] appreciate the outcome of my enterprises. At the end of two years, my property was distributed promiscuously throughout the State, and I was reduced to the necessity of making one final venture to recoup myself for the losses which, to the astonishment of the entire Texan community, I assured them I had met. I was the only man, as they asserted, 'that had ever failed to make a magnificent success in Texas.'

"You can readily conceive, gentlemen, that I was determined to make no mistake in my final venture. There were other reasons, beside the one of caution, which persuaded me to begin with a moderate investment; so I bought one cow. It was impossible for me to make a mistake from such a beginning. Every person in Texas that had rapidly risen to financial eminence had started with one cow. Many a time had a Texan ranchman swept his hand with a royal gesture over a landscape of flowers and Mesquite brush, dotted with thousands of cattle, and exclaimed, 'Stranger, I started this yer [Pg 26] ranch with one cow.' And then he would take out a piece of chalk and figure out to me on his saddle how that one cow had multiplied herself into seven thousand five hundred and twenty-three other cows, which had proceeded to promptly multiply themselves, 'regular as the seasons come round, sir,' in the same reckless manner, until it was evident that the number of her progeny was actually curtailed by the size of the saddle and the lack of chalk. Now, I was eager to possess a cow with such a multiplication-table attachment, and, being unable to wait even ten years before I could tingle with the sensation of being a millionnaire ranchman. I decided to shorten the probationary stage by half, and so I purchased two cows."

At this point, Dick rolled over upon the grass, and the major was doubled up as with sudden pain. As for myself, I confess I could not restrain my emotions. I had been through the same experience as had fallen to my guest, and I appreciated the sanguine characteristics [Pg 27] of his temperament, which prompted him to the investment, and the humor of the situation. I laughed till my eyes flowed with tears, and the stillness of the foot-hills resounded with the unrestrained merriment of the entire camp.

The humor of our guest was truly American, the humor of suggestive restraint and exaggeration both. He narrated his experiences, which had resulted in the loss of his fortune and the collapse of his hopes, with a face like a deacon's, and with a quaint and most charming sense of the ludicrousness of the position—a position of which he himself was the cause and central object. He fairly represented that type of men who combine in their composition that which is most practical and imaginative alike; whose energy can subdue a continent, and whose boastfulness would awaken contempt if it were not palliated by the magnitude of their achievements. A humor that is often barbed, but which is most willingly directed against one's self; but, whether directed against the humorist [Pg 28] or his neighbor, carries no poison upon its point and leaves no wound to rankle.

"My financial condition," said our guest, resuming, "my financial condition at the time I made this final investment contributed to the hopefulness of my mood, and made me feel the excitement of a reckless speculation, for, though my two cows only cost me seventeen dollars and fifty cents each, nevertheless, when the purchase was concluded, and the goods delivered, and I had made a careful inventory of my remaining assets,—a business proceeding which the average Texan found it necessary to go through about once in two weeks, in order that he might know what his financial standing was, or whether he had any standing at all,—when, I say, the purchase was consummated, and an inventory of my remaining assets made, I discovered that the two cows had swallowed up nearly my entire estate, and that a few dollars of farther expenditure would plunge me into bottomless insolvency. I must confess that [Pg 29] this disclosure of my financial condition added zest to the undertaking, and filled me with that fine excitement which accompanies a desperate speculation. I have always felt that another cow would have made a financier of me, and that I could have taken my place among my brethren in Wall Street without a tremor of the muscles or the least sense of inferiority.

"The cows were both black in color; so black that they would make a spot in the darkness of the blackest night that ever gloomed under the cypresses of the Guadaloupe. 'If those cows,' I said to myself as I looked them over, 'if those cows ever do bring forth calves at the rate that the Texan of whom I purchased them figured out on his saddle, they'll put the whole State under an eclipse.'

"I cannot say,—speaking with that restraint which I have always cultivated,—I cannot say, ladies and gentlemen, that I regarded either cow with any great affection. There were peculiarities about them, which checked the [Pg 30] outgoing of my emotional nature. They had a way of looking at me through the wire fence, that made me feel grateful to the inventor of barbed wire. I cannot describe the look exactly. It was a direct, earnest, steady, intense inspection of my person, that made me feel out of place, as it were, and caused me to remember that I had duties at home, which required me to get there as rapidly as possible.

"One morning, seeing that the basis of my speculation was near the centre of the field, and busily feeding on the bountiful growths of nature, I crept softly through the wires of the fence that I might gather some pecan nuts under a big tree that stood some twenty rods away. I reached the tree in safety, and proceeded to pick up the nuts. I had filled one pocket only when I heard a noise behind me, and, looking up, I saw that all the profits of my stock speculation, and all my stock itself, were coming toward me on a jump. I was never more collected in my life. My mind instantly [Pg 31] reached the conclusion that the pecan crop that year was so large in Texas that it would not pay to pick up another nut under that tree; that the whole thing should stand over, as it were, until another fall, and that, the sooner I retired from that field, the better it would be for me and the few pecans I had about me.

"Acting in harmony with this conclusion,—which to my mind carried with it the force of a demonstration,—I started for the wire fence. I have no doubt but that the line of my movement was absolutely straight. I assure you, gentlemen, that if cows had multiplied in my business connection as rapidly as they did in my imagination during the next sixty seconds of time, I should have been in Texas to this day. The whole field was actually alive with cows. I reached the fence just one jump ahead of the oldest cow, and, seeing no reason why I should take time to crawl through between the wires, I lifted myself over the airy obstruction in a manner that must have convinced that old [Pg 32] animated bit of blackness that I had absolute ownership in every nut about me. This little episode supplied me with material for reflection for at least a week, and made me realize that any northern man that enters into a speculation with Texas cows as a basis must keep his eyes open, and not allow his thoughts to be diverted by any side issues, like pecan nuts, while the business is developing.

"The sixth morning after my speculation had arrived at the ranch, my profits began to roll in upon me,—or, to state it more practically, and in a business-like manner, the oldest cow produced a calf. This raised my spirits, and made me feel that my business was fairly started. I went to my stock-book and promptly made an entry as follows: 7523-1. This meant that there were only seven thousand five hundred and twenty-*two* yet to realize on; that is, if seven thousand five hundred and twenty-two calves should promptly come to time, seeing that one calf had already actually come to time, my herd [Pg 33] would be complete. I think, gentlemen, you can readily understand my feelings as I stood contemplating the first fruition of my hopes from behind a tree. The cow was securely tied, but still from habit I took my usual position when inspecting my stock. My mood was very hopeful. I felt as every Texan felt, in those days, when by some accident he found himself in possession of actual property. 'There is a calf,' I said; 'I've only had to wait six days for that calf to materialize. Suppose another calf should materialize in six days.' I extracted a pencil from my pocket and began to figure. I multiplied that calf by six—I mean that at the end of six days I multiplied that calf by another calf. Every time I put down a new multiplier I took a look at the calf, and every time I looked at the calf it multiplied itself, as it were, until I felt the full force of the Texan's statement, save that, the more I multiplied, the more I felt that seven thousand five hundred and twenty-three did not fairly represent the [Pg 34] certainties of the speculation. That cow would surely make a millionnaire of me yet—if nothing happened.

"But, gentleman, something did happen, and it happened in this wise: You have doubtless, by this, concluded that the cow was a wild cow. The man who sold her to me had not put it precisely that way. He had represented her to me as a cow of mild manners, thoroughly domesticated, of the sweetest possible temper, used to the women folks, playful with children,—in short, a creature of such amiability that she actually longed to be petted. But I had already discovered that her manners were somewhat abrupt, and that either the man did not understand the nature of the cow or I did not understand the man. I was convinced that, if she had ever been domesticated, it had been done by some family every member of which had died in the process, or had suddenly moved out of the country only a short distance ahead of her, and that she had utterly forgotten her early [Pg 35] training. Still, I had no doubt but that her amiability was there, although temporarily somewhat latent, and that the influences of a gentle spirit would revive the dormant sensibilities of her nature. 'The sight of a milk-pail,' I said to myself, 'will surely awaken the reminiscences of her early days, and of that sweet home-life which was hers when she yielded at morn and at night her glad contribution to the nourishment of a Christian family.'

"There was on my ranch a servitor of foreign extraction who did my cooking for what he could eat,—Chin Foo by name,—and to him I called to bring me the large tin pail, which served the household—which, like most Texan households in the Tertiary period, so to speak, of their fortunes, was conducted on economic principles— as a washtub, a chip-basket, a water-bucket, and a dinner-gong. It also occurred to me, as I stood looking at the cow and caught the spirit of her expression, so to speak, that, as she had come to stay, was a [Pg 36] permanent fixture of the establishment, as it were, Chin Foo might as well do the milking first as last. Moreover, as the Texan from whom I purchased her had assured me that she was a kind of household pet, the children's friend, and took to women folks naturally, the case was a very clear one. For, as Chin Foo had long hair, wore no hat, and dressed in flowing drapery, the cow, unless she was more of a physiologist than I gave her credit for, would be in doubt somewhat as to the sex of the Chinaman; and before she had time to ruminate upon it and reach a dead-sure conclusion, the milking would be over; and I would have scored the first point in the game, if she was a cow of ability, had any trumps, and was up to any tricks, as it were. So I told Chin Foo, as he approached with the pail in his hand, that the cow was a splendid milker, thoroughly domesticated, accustomed to Chinamen, and that he might have the honor of milking her first. I remarked, furthermore, that, [Pg 37] as everything about the place was new to her, and she was a little nervous, I would gently attract her attention in front, while he proceeded to extract the delicious fluid. I charged him, in addition, to remember that it was always the best policy to approach a cow of her temperament in a bold and indifferent manner, as if he had milked her all his life, and get down to business at once; and that any hesitation or show of nervousness on his part would tend to make her more nervous.

"I must say that Chin Foo acted in a highly creditable manner, considering he was in a strange land, and, to my certain knowledge, had no money laid by for funeral expenses; for, while I was stirring the dust and flourishing my stick in a desultory manner in front of the cow, to divert her mind, and keep her thoughts from wandering backward too directly, he fluttered boldly up to her, and laid firmly hold of two teats, with the familiarity of an old acquaintance." [Pg 38]

At this point of his narration the stranger paused a moment. There was a sort of plaintive look on his face, and he gazed at the plates with an expression in his eyes of sorrowful recollection.

"I cannot say," he resumed, as one who speaks oppressed with a sense of uncertainty, "exactly what did happen, for I never saw the Chinaman again until he alighted. I only know that when he came down he was practically inside the pail, and that he sat in it a moment with a kind of dreamy eastern look on his face, as if he lived on the isle of Patmos and had seen a vision. And when he had crawled out of the pail he went directly into the house, saying, 'The

Melican man is dam foolee to try to milkee that cussee!' or words to
that effect.

Practically Inside the Pail.

"But I did not agree with him. I reflected that the Chinese are only an imitative race, and wholly lacking in original perception. 'They never invent anything,' I said; 'never study [Pg 39] into causes, never get down to principles, as it were. It requires a purely occidental intellect to master the problem before me. This cow has a strong disinclination to be milked. Why? What is the motive of her conduct? If I could only answer that!' All at once it came to me,—came like a flash. The reason was plain. 'This cow is a mother. The maternal instinct in her case is beautifully developed. Her reasoning faculties less so. She has a calf. To her mind, we are trying to rob her beloved offspring of its nourishment. She naturally resents this injustice on our part. Beautiful development of maternity,' I apostrophized, as I looked at the cow in the light of this new revelation. 'Thy instincts are those that sweeten the world, and remind us of the benignity that planned the universe. I will bring thy calf to thee. I will show thee that I am not devoid of the spirit of equity; that I am ready to go shares and play fair, as it were. Thy calf shall take one side of thee. I [Pg 40] will take the other, and thy soul will come forth to me in gratitude!'

"I was delighted. I went directly to the pen, and gazed benevolently at the calf. The little imp was blacker, if possible, than its mother. There was that same peculiar look also in its eyes. 'You're all hers!' I joyfully cried, 'you are your mother's own child!' I seized hold of the neck-rope. I opened the pen-door and I went out through that door quicker than a vagrant cat ever got round a corner of a house where a Scotch terrier boards. The calf went under the cow and I struck her, head on. But I had come to stay. I grabbed the pail with one hand and a teat with the other. I tugged it, pulled it, twisted it. Not a drop could I start. A suction pump of twenty horse-power would have found it drier than Sahara, and all the while the calf's mouth, on the other side, was actually running over with milk! In two minutes he looked like a black watermelon. Then the cow, with a kind of back action, suddenly [Pg 41] reached out one foot, and when I came to I found myself facing a mulberry tree, with one leg on each side of it.

"And When I Came Down."

"By this time I had reached a decision, and I had the courage of my convictions. I felt it to be my duty to milk that cow. I reminded her in plain, straightforward language that I was the son of a deacon, and that she'd find it out before she got through with me. I assured her that I understood the beauty of righteousness, and that I held a strong hand—a straight flush, as it were. I was well aware that the metaphor was somewhat mixed; but it expressed my sentiments and relieved my feelings, and so I fired it at her point-blank. She snorted and pawed and bellowed, and swore at me in cow-language, but I didn't care for that. So I shook the old, battered milk-pail in her face, and told her I was born in Connecticut, and did business on spot-cash principle; and that she would know more of the commandments than any cow of her color in Texas, before we said our long farewell. [Pg 42]

"By this time the matter had attracted a good deal of attention, for I had carried on my conversation with the cow in the voice of a tragedian when the chief villain of the play has stolen his girl, and my next neighbor, an old sea-captain from Mattagorda Bay, and his hired men had come over to assist me. They were of the nature of a reënforcement, which consisted of the captain, a Mexican, a Michigan man that stuttered, and two negroes—Napoleon Bonaparte de Neville Smith, and George Washington Marlborough Johnsing, by name. Hence we were six in all, and I decided to take the offensive at once. The captain was advanced in years and rheumatic, but a clearheaded man, used to command, and had 'boarded,' as he expressed it, 'several of the— —crafts in his own waters.' So I put him in charge of the marines, namely, ourselves, and told him to fight the ship for all she was worth. He caught on to the thing at once, and swore he would 'sweep the old black hulk fore and [Pg 43] aft, and send every mother's son to the bottom, or make her strike her colors.' The vigor of the gallant old gentleman's language, and the noble manner in which he shook his cane at the old pirate, put us all in good spirits, and I verily believe that, if he had at that fortunate moment given the word 'board!' we would, niggers and all, have gone over the bulwarks of that old cow with a rush.

"The captain's plan of action was proof of his courage, and in harmony with my own ideas of the matter. He said that our force was ample, every gun shotted, and the ports open: that we had the windward gauge of her, and that the proper course was to send a boat in to cut her cable, and, when she drifted down with the current, we would ware ship, lay up alongside, grapple, pass lashings aboard, and send the whole crew on to her deck with a rush. Assaulted in such a man-of-war style, he was confident she would become confused, be intimidated, and strike her colors without firing [Pg 44] a gun. The brave and sonorous language with which our commander set forth his plan of assault captured our imaginations, and we all longed for the moment when the word of command should permit us to swarm up the sides and over the rail of the old bovine.

"Not only was the general plan thus agreed upon, but each man had his post of duty assigned to him. When the 'cable was cut,' that is, when the cow should find herself at liberty and bolt, as she would be sure to do, the Mexican was to lasso her and hang on; Napoleon Bonaparte de Neville and George Washington Marlborough were to lay hold of her horns to 'port and starboard,' as the captain insisted, while the Michigan man — who was over six feet tall, and leggy — was to fasten with a good grip on to her tail, that he might serve not only as a 'drag,' as our commander phrased it, but as a pilot as well, 'if she should get to yawing or be suddenly taken aback, and be unable to come up into the wind promptly,' [Pg 45] while I was held in reserve to guard against emergencies. I did not quite like the position assigned to me, and so intimated to the captain, but he said no one could tell how it might go when we once got out of the harbor, and, if any of the braces should part, or the sea get high, that he would have to send an additional man to the wheel, 'for,' he added, in a whisper, 'God knows, that long-legged Michigan land-lubber could never keep her to a straight course if she should once get running with the wind over her quarter, and everything drawing, through that cornfield.' I saw the force of his reasoning, and felt easier.

"So, without farther delay, we went into action. The old captain stood, knife in hand, ready to cut the lariat which held the cow to the tree, but, before he did so, he hailed, '*All ready to cut cables!*'

"'Fo' de lawd, cap'in!' yelled Napoleon de Neville, 'what is dis yere nigger gwine to do if de udder nigger lets go?' [Pg 46]

"'Go way dar, nigger!' retorted George Washington Marlborough; 'what you takes dis nigger for if you tinks I's gwine to let go dis ole black cow?'

"'I'll give a silver dollar to the nigger that holds on the longest,' I yelled.

"'Well answered, mate,' sang out the old captain. '*All ready to cut cables. Cut she is!*'

"The cow gave a bellow like the roar of a lion, and made a rush with lowered horns at the captain. Now, this was not the course laid down on his chart for her to take; and he and the rest of us were struck all aback, as he afterwards expressed it; but he met the emergency with spirit. He broke his big, Spanish-oak stick on the nose of the brute, and then the old mariner rolled in the dust.

"'Lay aboard of her, men!' shouted the old hero, in a voice like a fog-horn, flourishing the fragments of his stick. 'Lay aboard of the old cuss, I say! Cast your grapplings, [Pg 47] Greaser! Seize her helm, some of ye, and throw it hard over to port!'

"Lay Aboard of the Old Cuss!"

"These orders were obeyed with alacrity. Not a man flinched. The loop of the lasso settled over the polished horns to the roots, and Don Juan San Diego set it tight with a twang. Napoleon Bonaparte and George Washington rushed headlong upon her and hung to horns and ears; while the man from Michigan fastened a grip on her lifted tail, as she tore past him, which straightened him out like a lathe. As to myself, I could only stand and gaze with solicitude upon the terrific contest, on the issue of which depended not only the chances of my speculation, but even the preservation of my self-esteem.

"The combat deepened and enlarged itself, as it were. A bull-dog, who was wandering along the road in search of adventure, and two foxhounds joined in the fight. The calf, the only one of the seven thousand five hundred and twenty-three I was ever destined to behold, [Pg 48] broke from its pen and ran bellowing to its mother. The dogs bayed, the niggers yelled, the Mexican swore in his delightful tongue; and the stuttering Michigander remained silent, simply from his inability to pronounce the profanity of his feelings.

"Suddenly the cow, which had been slowly working her way, with her several attachments clinging to her, toward the road which ran along the front of the field, turned and started pell-mell toward the river, which flowed wide and deep, through the rushes, at the rear of it. She left the path and took to the corn, and through the mass of growing stalks she swept like a whirlwind. Onward she came. I anticipated the awful catastrophe, and stood riveted to the spot. The old captain still sat in the gravel, where the cow had bowled him, his hand grasping the shattered cane, and his game leg extended. He too foresaw the inevitable. Through the corn came the cow, like a black Saturn attended by her satellites. But her [Pg 49] career was too terrific for these to hold to their connection. The laws of the universe forbade it. Napoleon Bonaparte de Neville lost his hold as she crashed into the sorghum patch. George Washington Marlborough tripped over an irrigation ditch, and soared away at a tangent, like a sputtering remnant of a burnt-out world. Don Juan San Diego went the wrong side of a mulberry tree, and the lasso parted with a snap. He never stopped until his momentum carried him through the slats of the neighboring cow-pen. Only the long-legged Michigander kept his hold, and he looked like a pair of extended scissors. I stood aghast at the impending ruin of my hopes, with my lower jaw dropped. The captain alone retained his presence of mind. As the black unit of my last Texan speculation shot by him, with Michigan, elongated like a peninsula, fastened to her tail, he rolled up to his knees and roared: —

[Pg 50]

"'*Starboard your helm, boy! Luff her up! Luff her up, for the love of God, or the colonel is busted!*'

"It is doubtful if the Michigan man ever heard the stentorian call of the captain, for sound travels only thirteen hundred feet to the second, and the cow was certainly going considerably faster than that; and, besides, he was himself engaged, with a terrific earnestness, in a vain effort to extricate a word out of his throat, which stuck like a wad in a smutty gun—a word of undoubted Saxon origin and of expressive force, and which has saved more blood-vessels from bursting than the lancet of the phlebotomist, for as he streamed past there was left floating upon the air a long string of d's, thus: d − −d − −d−d−d−d-d-d...!

"No one who did not hear them could ever conceive of the awful sputtering, hissing sound that they caused in the atmosphere as they came out of the mouth of the mad and stuttering Michigander; and as he and the cow bored a hole through the reeds on the bank of the [Pg 51] river, and, hitting a cypress stump, ricochetted into the water, that fiery string of d's, still hot and sputtering, reached half across the field.

"Luff Her Up! Luff Her Up!"

"The splash of the two as they struck the water brought the old captain to his feet, and, in spite of his rheumatic leg, he rushed toward the river, crying:—

"'*Man overboard! Man overboard! Gone clean over the forechains! Life-floats to port and starboard!'*

"With such a frightful catastrophe, gentlemen, the remembrance of which actually makes me nervous, my last speculation in Texas ended. Going over the whole matter with the captain that evening,—a process which took us well into the night,—it was our united opinion that the speculation was a failure. This conviction was mutual and profound. The cow was not only gone, but she had shown such disinclination to be domesticated, and such a misapprehension of the true purpose of life, that the prospect was truly disheartening. [Pg 52]

"'Why, damn it, colonel,' said the captain, 'we've no evidence that the old cow wanted to be milked!'

"To this discouraging conclusion of the captain's I was compelled to give a sorrowful assent. I recognized that my speculation was in arrears, as it were, and that it would never figure up a profit.

"Therefore, next day I divided my few personal effects between the captain and the noble men who had risked their lives for an idea; who had seen the tragedy played out and the curtain rung down to my last appearance, as it were. And, with the few dollars which alone remained of the fortune which I took with me to Texas, I mounted my horse and started northward, to join that noble army of martyrs, that brotherhood of sufferers, that fraternity of the busted, whose members are legion, and who are known as '*Ex-Texans.*'"

The hilarity of the camp that evening under the foot-hills will never be forgotten by those of us who composed the happy number, and who [Pg 53] listened with streaming eyes and aching sides to the narrative of our unfortunate guest. He told his story with a directness and simplicity of narrative, with a gravity of countenance and plaintiveness of voice, which heightened the humor of the substance. Never did the stars, which have seen so much of human happiness, which have listened to so much of the rollicking humor of those who were fashioned for laughter, looked down upon a jollier camp. Long after our guest had ended his narrative and was apparently sleeping in happy forgetfulness of his Texas speculation, succeeding pauses of silence would come roars of laughter. The remembrance of the humorous tale banished sleep, and, even after slumber had fallen on us all, fun still held possession of our dreams. For Dick, starting from sleep in a nightmare of hilarity, roared out: *"Luff her up, luff her up, or the colonel is busted!"*

Ay, ay, thank God for laughter. Thank him heartily and ever, dear friend, blow the winds, run the tides as they may. The sorrows [Pg 54] of life may be many, and its griefs may be keen, and we who are frosted with years and you who are blooming have felt and will feel the sting of false friends and the burden of losses; but, lose what we may, or be pained as we have been and shall be, we are happy in this, — we who know how to laugh, — that we find wings for each burden, solace for pains, and return for all losses, in our sweet sense of humor, thank Heaven! So, whether rich men or poor, healthy or sick, brown-headed or gray, we will go on like children, with eyes for all beauty and hearts for all fun. Let lilies teach us, and of the birds of the air let us learn. The day that is not shall not make us anxious, for of each day is the evil enough, and the morrow shall take care of itself.

[Pg 55]

HOW DEACON TUBMAN AND PARSON WHITNEY CELEBRATED NEW YEAR'S.

"Mirandy, I'm going up to see the parson," exclaimed the deacon, when the morning devotions were over, "and see if I can thaw him out a little. I've heard that there used to be a lot in him in his younger days, but he's sort of frozen all up latterly, and I can see that the young folks are afraid of him and the church too, but that won't do—no, it won't do," repeated the good man emphatically, "for the minister ought to be loved by young and old, rich and poor, and everybody; and a church without young folks in it is, why, it is like a family with no children in it. Yes, I'll go up and wish him a Happy New Year anyway. [Pg 56] Perhaps I can get him out for a ride to make some calls on the people, and see the young folks at their fun. It'll do him good, and them good, and me good, and everybody good." Saying which, the deacon got inside his warm fur coat, and started toward the barn to harness Jack into the worn, old-fashioned sleigh, which sleigh was built high in the back, and had a curved dasher of monstrous proportions, ornamented with a prancing horse in an impossible attitude, done in bright vermilion on a blue background!

"Happy New Year to you, Parson Whitney! Happy New Year to you," cried the deacon, as he stood in the doorway of the parsonage and shook the parson by the hand enthusiastically, "and may you live to enjoy a hundred."

"Come in, come in," cried Parson Whitney, in response. "I'm glad you've come; I'm glad you've come. I've been wanting to see you all the morning," and in the cordiality of his greeting he literally pulled the little man through the [Pg 57] doorway into the hall, and hurried him up the stairway to his study in the chamber overhead.

"Thinking of me! Well, now, I never!" exclaimed the deacon, as, assisted by the parson, he twisted and wriggled himself out of his coat, that he filled, a little too snugly for an easy exit. "Thinking of me, and among all these books too—Bibles, catechisms, tracts, theologies, sermons. Well, well, that is funny. What made you think of me?"

"Deacon Tubman," responded the parson, as he seated himself in his armchair, "I want to talk with you about the church."

"The church!" ejaculated the deacon in response. "Nothing going wrong, I hope?"

"Yes, things are going wrong, deacon," responded the parson. "The congregation is growing smaller and smaller, and yet I preach good, strong, biblical, soul-satisfying sermons, I trust."

"Good ones! good ones!" answered the deacon promptly, "never better—never better in the world." [Pg 58]

"And yet the people are deserting the sanctuary," rejoined the parson solemnly, "and the young people won't come to the sociables, and the little children seem actually afraid of me. What shall I do, deacon?" and the good man put the question with pathetic emphasis.

"You've hit the nail on the head, square as a hatchet, parson," responded the deacon. "The congregation is thinning. The young people don't come to the meetings, and the little children are afraid of you."

"What's the matter, deacon?" cried the parson in return. "What is it?" he repeated earnestly. "Speak it right out; don't try to spare my feelings. I will listen to—I will do anything to win back my people's love," and the strong, old-fashioned Calvinistic preacher said it in a voice that actually trembled.

"You can do it—you can do it in a week!" exclaimed the deacon encouragingly. "Don't worry about it, parson; it'll be all right, it'll be all right. Your books are the trouble." [Pg 59]

"Books?" ejaculated the parson. "What have they to do with it?"

"Everything," replied the deacon stoutly. "You pore over them day in and day out; they keep you in this room here when you should be out among the people,—not making pastoral visits,—I don't mean that,—but going around among them, chatting and joking and having a good time. They would like it, and you would like it, and as for the young folks—how old are you, parson?"

"Sixty next month," answered the parson; "sixty next month," he repeated solemnly.

"Thirty! thirty! that's all you are, parson, or all you ought to be," cried the deacon. "Thirty, twenty, sixteen!—let the figures slide down and up, according to circumstances, but never let them go higher than thirty when you are dealing with young folks. I'm sixty myself, counting years; but I'm only sixteen, sixteen this morning, that's all, parson," and he rubbed his little round plump hands together, looked at the parson, and winked. [Pg 60]

"Bless my soul, Deacon Tubman, I don't know but that you are right!" answered the parson. "Sixty? I don't know as I am sixty," and he began to rub his own hands, and came within an ace of executing a wink at the deacon, himself.

"Not a day over twenty, if I am any judge of age," responded the deacon deliberately, as he looked the white-headed old minister over with a most comic imitation of seriousness. "Not a day over twenty, on my honor," and the deacon leaned forward toward the parson, and gave him a punch with his thumb, as one boy might deliver a punch at another, and then he lay back in his chair and laughed so heartily that the parson caught the infectious mirth and roared away as heartily as himself.

Yes, it was impossible to sit hobnobbing with the little, jolly deacon on that bright New Year's morning and not be affected by the happiness of his mood, for he was actually bubbling over with fun, and as full of frolic as if the finger [Pg 61] on the dial had, in truth, gone back forty-odd years, and he was "only sixteen. Only sixteen, parson, on my honor."

"But what can I do?" queried the good man, sobering down. "I make my pastoral visits."

"Pastoral visits!" responded Deacon Tubman. "Oh, yes, and they are all well enough for the old folks, but they ar'n't the kind of biscuit the young folks like—too heavy in the centre, and over-hard in the crust for young teeth, eh, parson?"

"But what shall I do? what shall I do?" reiterated the parson, somewhat despondently.

"Oh! put on your hat, and gloves, and warmest coat, and come along with me. We will see what the young folks are doing, and will make a day of it. Come! come! let the old books, and catechisms, and sermons, and tracts have a respite for once, and we'll spend the day out-of-doors, with the boys and girls and the people." [Pg 62]

"I'll do it!" exclaimed the parson. "Deacon Tubman, you are right. I do keep to my study too closely. I don't see enough of the world and what's going on in it. I was reading the Testament this morning, and I was impressed with the Master's manner of living and teaching. It is not certain that he ever preached more than twice in a church during all his ministry on the earth. And the children! how much he loved the children, and how the little ones loved him! And why shouldn't they love me, too? Why shouldn't they? I'll make them do it! yes, I'll make them do it! The lambs of my flock shall love me." And with these brave words Parson Whitney bundled himself up in his warmest garments, and followed the deacon downstairs.

"Tell the folks that you won't be back till night," called the deacon from the sleigh; "for this is New Year, and we're going to make a day of it," and he laughed away as heartily as might be—so heartily that the par [Pg 63] son joined in the laughter himself as he came shuffling down the icy path toward him. "Bless me! how much younger I feel already!" said the good man as he stood up in the sleigh, and with a long, strong breath breathed the cool, pure air into his lungs. "Bless me! how much younger I feel already!" he repeated, as he settled down into the roomy seat of the old sleigh. "Only sixteen to-day,—eh, deacon?" and he nudged him with his elbow.

"That's all, that's all, parson," answered the deacon gayly, as he nudged him vigorously back; "that's all we are, either of us," and, laughing as merrily as two boys, the two glided away in the sleigh.

Well, perhaps they didn't have fun that day, these two old boys that had started out with the feeling that they were "only sixteen," and bound to make "a day of it!" And they did make a day of it, in fact, and such a day as neither had had for forty years; for, first, they went to Bartlett's Hill, where the boys and [Pg 64] girls were coasting, and coasted with them for a full hour,—and then it was discovered by the younger portion of his flock that the parson was not an old, stiff, solemn, surly poke, as they had thought, but a pleasant, good-natured, kindly soul, who could take and give a joke, and steer a sled as well as the smartest boy in the crowd; and when it came to snow-balling, he could send a ball further than Bill Sykes himself, who could out-throw any boy in town, and roll up a bigger block to the new snow fort they were building than any three boys among them. And how the parson enjoyed being a boy again! How exhilarating the slide down the steep hill; how invigorating the pure, cool air; how pleasant the noise of the chatting and joking going on around him; how bright and sweet the boys and girls looked, with their rosy cheeks and sparkling eyes; and how the old parson's heart thrilled as they crowded around him when he would go, and urged him to stay,—and little Alice Dor [Pg 65] chester begged him, with her little arms around his neck, to "jes' stay and gib me one more slide, please!"

"You never made such a pastoral call as that, parson," said the deacon, as they drove away amid the cheers of the boys and the "good-bys" of the girls, while the former fired off a volley of snow-balls in his honor, and the latter waved their muffs and handker-chiefs after them.

"God bless them! God bless them!" said the parson. "They have lifted a load from my heart, and taught me the sweetness of life, of youth, and the wisdom of Him who took the little ones in His arms, and blessed them. Ah, deacon," he added, "I've been a great fool, but I'll be so, thank God! no more."

Now, old Jack was a horse of a great deal of character, and had a great history; but of this none in that section, save the little deacon, knew a word. Dick Tubman, the deacon's youngest, wildest, and, we might add, favorite [Pg 66] son, had purchased him of an impe-cunious jockey, at the close of a disastrous campaign, that cleaned him completely out, and left him in a strange city a thousand miles from home, with nothing but the horse, harness, and sulky, and a list of unpaid bills that must be met before he could leave the scene of his disastrous fortunes. Under such circumstances it was that Dick Tubman ran across the horse, and partly out of pity for its owner, and partly out of admiration of the horse, whose failure to win at the races was due more to his lack of condition and the bad management of his jockey than lack of speed, bought him off-hand, and, having no use for him himself, shipped him as a present to the deacon, with whom he had now been four years, with no harder work than ploughing out the good old man's corn in the summer, and jogging along the country roads on the deacon's errands. Having said thus much of the horse, perhaps we should more particularly describe him. [Pg 67]

He was, in sooth, an animal of most unique and extraordinary appearance; for, in the first place, he was quite seventeen hands in height, and long in proportion. He was also the reverse of shapely in the fashion of his build: for his head was long and bony, and his hip bones sharp and protuberant; his tail was what is known among horsemen as a rat-tail, being but scantily covered with hair, and his neck was even more scantily supplied with a mane, while in color he could easily have taken any premium put up for homeliness, being an ashen roan, mottled with flecks and patches of divers hues; but his legs were flat and corded like a racer's, his neck long and thin as a thoroughbred's, his nostrils large, his ears sharply pointed and lively, while the white rings around his eyes hinted at a cross, somewhere in his pedigree, with Arabian blood. A huge, bony, homely-looking horse he was, who drew the deacon and Miranda into the village on market days and Sundays, with a loose, shambling gait, making [Pg 68] altogether an appearance so homely and peculiar that the smart village chaps riding along in their jaunty turn-outs used to chaff the good deacon on the character of his steed, and satirically challenge him to a brush. The deacon always took their badinage in good part, although he inwardly said more than once, "If I ever get a good chance, when there ar'n't too many around, I'll go up to the turn of the road beyond the church, and let Jack out on them;" for Dick had given him a hint of the horse's history, and told him "he could knock the spots out of thirty," and wickedly urged the deacon to take the starch out of them airy chaps some of these days. Such was the horse, then, that the deacon had ahead of him, and the old-fashioned sleigh, when, with the parson alongside, he struck into the principal street of the village.

Now, New Year's Day is a lively day in many country villages, and on this bright one especially, as the sleighing was perfect, everybody [Pg 69] was out. Indeed, it had got noised abroad that certain trotters of local fame were to be on the street that afternoon, and, as the boys worded it, "there would be heaps of fun going on."

And so it happened that everybody in town, and many who lived out of it, were on this particular street, and just at the hour, too, when the deacon came to the foot of it, so that the walk on either side was lined darkly with lookers-on, and the smooth snow-path between the two lines looked like a veritable homestretch on a race-day.

Now, when the deacon had reached the corner of the main street and turned into it, it was at that point where the course terminated and the "brushes" were ended, and at the precise moment when the dozen or twenty horses that had just come flying down were being pulled up preparatory to returning at a slow gait to the customary starting-point at the head of the street, a half-mile away, so that the old-fashioned sleigh was surrounded by the [Pg 70] light, fancy cutters of the rival racers, and old Jack was shambling awkwardly along in the midst of the high-spirited and smoking nags that had just come flying down the stretch.

"Hellow, deacon," shouted one of the boys, who was driving a trim-looking bay, and who had crossed the line at the ending of the course second only to a pacer that could "speed like a streak of lightning," as the boys said, — "Hellow, deacon; ain't you going to shake out old shamble-heels, and show us fellows what speed is to-day?" And the merry-hearted chap, son of the principal lawyer of the place, laughed heartily at his challenge, while the other drivers looked at the great angular horse that, without any check, was walking carelessly along, with his head held down, ahead of the old sleigh and its churchly occupants.

"I don't know but what I will," answered the deacon, good-naturedly; "don't know but what I will, if the parson don't object, and you won't start off too quick to begin with; for this is [Pg 71] New Year's, and a little extra fun won't hurt any of us, I reckon."

The Deacon and Parson.

"Do it, do it; we'll hold up for you," answered a dozen merry voices. "Do it, deacon: it'll do old shamble-heels good to go a ten-mile-an-hour gait for once in his life, and the parson needn't fear of being scandalized by any speed you'll get out of him, either;" and the merry chaps haw-hawed as men and boys will, when every one is jolly and fun flows fast.

And so, with any amount of good-natured chaffing from the drivers of the "fast 'uns," and from many that lined the road too,—for the day gave greater liberty than usual to bantering speech,—the speedy ones paced slowly up to the head of the street, with old Jack shambling demurely in the midst of them.

But the horse was a knowing old fellow, and had "scored" at too many races not to know that the "return" was to be leisurely taken, and, indeed, he was a horse of independence, and of too even, per-haps of too sluggish, a [Pg 72] temperament, to waste himself in needless action; but he had the right stuff in him, and hadn't forgot-ten his early training either, for when he came to the "turn," his head and tail came up, his eye brightened, and, with a playful movement of his huge body, and without the least hint from the deacon, he swung himself and the cumbrous old sleigh into line, and began to straighten himself for the coming brush.

45

Now, Jack was, as we have said, a horse of huge proportions, and needed "steadying" at the start, but the good deacon had no experience with the "ribbons," and was therefore utterly unskilled in the matter of driving; and so it came about that old Jack was so confused at the start that he made a most awkward and wretched appearance in his effort to get off, being all "mixed up," as the saying is,—so much so that the crowd roared at his ungainly efforts, and his flying rivals were twenty rods away before he even got started. But at last [Pg 73] he got his huge body in a straight line, and, leaving his miserable shuffle, squared away to his work, and, with head and tail up, went off at so slashing a gait that it fairly took the deacon's breath away, and caused the crowd that had been hooting him to roar their applause, while the parson grabbed the edge of the old sleigh with one hand and the rim of his tall black hat with the other.

What a pity, Mr. Longface, that God made horses as they are, and gave them such grandeur of appearance when in action, and put such an eagle-like spirit between their ribs, so that, quitting the plodding motions of the ox, they can fly like that noble bird, and come sweeping down the course as on wings of the wind!

It was not my fault, nor the deacon's, nor the parson's either, please remember, then, that awkward, shuffling, homely-looking old Jack was thus suddenly transformed, by the royalty of blood, of pride, and of speed given him by [Pg 74] his Creator, from what he ordinarily was, into a magnificent spectacle of energetic velocity.

With muzzle lifted well up, tail erect, the few hairs in it streaming straight behind, one ear pricked forward and the other turned sharply back, the great horse swept grandly along at a pace that was rapidly bringing him even with the rear line of the flying group. And yet so little was the pace to him that he fairly gambolled in playfulness as he went slashing along, until the deacon verily began to fear that the honest old chap would break through all the bounds of propriety and send his heels antically through his treasured dashboard. Indeed, the spectacle that the huge horse presented was so magnificent, his action so free, spirited, and playful, as he came sweeping onward, that cheers and exclamations, such as, "Good heavens! see the deacon's old horse!" "Look at him! look at him!" "What a stride!" etc., ran ahead of him, and old Bill Sykes, a trainer in his day, but now a hanger-on at the village [Pg 75] tavern, or that section of it known as the bar, wiped his watery eyes with his tremulous fist, as he saw Jack come swinging down, and, as he swept past with his open gait, powerful stroke, and stiffles playing well out, brought his hand with a mighty slap against his thigh, and said, "I'll be blowed if he isn't a regular old timer!"

It was fortunate for the deacon and the parson that the noise and cheering of the crowd drew the attention of the drivers ahead, or there would surely have been more than one collision, for the old sleigh was of such size and strength, the good deacon so unskilled at the reins, and Jack, who was adding to his momentum with every stride, was going at so determined a pace, that, had he struck the rear line, with no gap for him to go through, something serious would surely have happened. But, as it was, the drivers saw the huge horse, with the cumbrous old sleigh behind him, bearing down on them at such a gait as made their own speed, sharp as it was, seem slow, and "pulled out" in time [Pg 76] to save themselves; and so without any mishap the big horse and heavy sleigh swept through the rear row of racers like an autumn gust through a cluster of leaves.

By this time the deacon had become somewhat alarmed, for Jack was going nigh to a thirty clip,—a frightful pace for an inexperienced man to ride,—and began to put a good strong pressure upon the bit, not doubting that old Jack—ordinarily the easiest horse in the world to manage—would take the hint and immediately slow up. But though the huge horse took the hint, it was exactly in the opposite manner that the deacon intended he should, for he interpreted the little man's steady pull as an intimation that his inexperienced driver was getting over his flurry and beginning to treat him as a big horse ought to be treated in a race, and that he could now, having got settled to his work, go ahead. And go ahead he did. The more the deacon pulled, the more the great horse felt himself steadied [Pg 77] and assisted. And so, the harder the good man tugged at the reins, the more powerfully the machinery of the big animal ahead of him worked, until the deacon got alarmed, and began to call upon the horse to stop, crying, "Whoa, Jack! whoa, old boy, I say! Whoa, will you now, that's a good fellow!" and many other coaxing calls, while he pulled away steadily at the reins.

But the horse misunderstood the deacon's calls, as he had his pressure on the reins, for the crowd on either side were now yelling, and hooting, and swinging their caps, so that the deacon's voice came indistinctly to his ears at the best, and he interpreted his calls for him to stop as only so many encouragements and signals for him to go ahead; and so, with the memory of a hundred races stirring his blood, the crowd cheering him to the echo, the steadying pull and encouraging cries of his driver in his ears, and his only rival, the pacer, whirling along only a few rods ahead of him, the mon [Pg 78] strous animal, with a desperate plunge that half lifted the old sleigh from the snow, let out another link, and, with such a burst of speed as was never seen in the village before, tore along after the pacer at such a terrific pace that, within the distance of a dozen lengths, he lay lapped upon him, and the two were going it nose and nose.

What is that feeling in human hearts which makes us sympathetic with man or animal who has unexpectedly developed courage and capacity when engaged in a struggle in which the odds are against him? And why do we enter so spiritedly into the contest, and lose ourselves in the excitement of the moment? Is it pride? Is it the comradeship of courage? Or is it the rising of the indomitable in us, that loves nothing so much as victory, and hates nothing so much as defeat? Be that as it may, no sooner was old Jack fairly lapped on the pacer, whose driver was urging him along with reins and voice alike, and the contest seemed doubtful, [Pg 79] than the spirit of old Adam himself entered into the deacon and the parson both, so that, carried away by the excitement of the race, they fairly forgot themselves, and entered as wildly into the contest as two ungodly jockeys.

The Race.

"Deacon Tubman!" said the parson, as he clutched the rim of his tall hat, against which, as the horse tore along, the snow chips were pelting in showers, more stoutly, "Deacon Tubman! do you think the pacer will beat us?"

"Not if I can help it! not if I can help it!" yelled the deacon in reply, as, with something like a reinsman's skill, he instinctively lifted Jack to another spurt. "Go it, old boy!" he shouted encouragingly. "Go along with you, I say!" and the parson, also carried away by the whirl of the moment, cried, "Go along, old boy! Go along with you, I say!"

This was the very thing, and the only thing, that huge horse, whose blood was now fairly aflame, wanted to rally him for the final effort; and, in response to the encouraging cries of the two [Pg 80] behind him, he gathered himself together for another burst of speed, and put forth his collected strength with such tremendous energy and suddenness of movement that the little deacon, who had risen, and was standing erect in the sleigh, fell back into the arms of the parson, while the great horse rushed over the line a winner by a clear length, amid such cheers and roars of laughter as were never heard in that village before.

Nor was the horse any more the object of public interest and remark—we may say favoring remark—than the parson, who suddenly found himself the centre of a crowd of his own parishioners, many of whom would scarcely be expected as participants of such a scene, but who, thawed out of their iciness by the genial temper of the day, and vastly excited over Jack's contest, thronged upon the good man, laughing as heartily as any jolly sinner in the crowd.

So everybody shook hands with the parson [Pg 81] and wished him a Happy New Year, and the parson shook hands with everybody and wished them all many happy returns; and everybody praised old Jack, and rallied the deacon on his driving; and then everybody went home good-natured and happy, laughing and talking about the wonderful race, and the change that had come over Parson Whitney.

And as for Parson Whitney himself, the day and its fun had taken twenty years from his age, and nothing would answer but the deacon must go home and eat the New Year's pudding at the parsonage; and he did. And at the table they laughed and talked over the funny incidents of the day, and joked each other as merrily as two boys. Then Parson Whitney told some reminiscences of his college days, and the scrapes he got into, and a riot between town and gown, when he carried the "Bully's Club;" and the deacon responded by narrating his experiences with a certain Deacon Jones's watermelon patch when he was a boy, and over [Pg 82] their tales and their mulled cider they laughed till they cried, and roared so lustily at the remembered frolics of their youthful days that the old parsonage rang, the books on the library shelves rattled, and several of the theological volumes actually gaped with horror.

But at last the stories were all told, the jokes all cracked, and the laughter all laughed, and the little deacon wished the parson good-by, and jogged happily homeward; but more than once he laughed to himself, and said, "Bless my soul! I didn't know the parson had so much fun in him." And long the parson sat by the glowing grate after the deacon had left him, musing of other days, and the happy, pleasant things that were in them; and many times he smiled, and once he laughed outright at some remembered folly, for he said,

"What a wild boy I was, and yet I meant no wrong; and the dear old days were very happy."

Ay, ay! Parson Whitney, the dear old days were very happy, not only to thee, but to all of [Pg 83] us, who, following our sun, have fared westward so long that the light of the morning shows dull through the dim haze of memory. But happier than even the old days will be the young ones, I ween, when, following still westward, we suddenly come to the gates of the new east and the morning once more; and there, in the dawn of a day which is cloudless and endless, we find our lost youth and its loves, to lose them and it no more forever, thank God! [Pg 84]

[Pg 85]

THE LEAF OF RED ROSE:

THE OLD TRAPPER'S STORY.

A story? Why, yes. If Henry, there, will translate it
And put it in verse and print as he promised
To do when it happened. Will he do it? I doubt.
He dislikes to dabble with rhyme and with measure.
Says that good honest prose is the best and the sweetest
If the words be well chosen, short, Saxon, and pithy.
And that making of verse is the business of women,
[Pg 86] Of green boys at school, and of lovers when spooning.
But try him. It may be he will. For a lesson
Is in it, and that makes it worth telling.
The woods have their secrets and sorrows and struggles
As well as the cities. You can find in the woods
Many things, if you look, beside trees, rocks, and mountains.

Jack Whitcomb he said his name was, though I doubted.
For the name on his bosom, tattooed in purple,
Didn't point quite that way. But that doesn't matter.
One name in the woods is as good as another
If a man answers to it and it's easily spoken.
So we called him Jack Whitcomb and asked nothing further.

[Pg 87] Brave? Why, of course he was brave. Men are not cowards.
Cowards don't come to the woods. They stay in the cities,
Where policemen are thick and the streets are all lighted.
In the woods men trail with their ears and eyes open,
And sleep when they sleep with their hands on their rifles.
Why? Well, panthers are plenty and cunning and quiet,
And a man is a fool that goes carelessly stumbling
Under trees where they crouch, under crags where they gather.
Furthermore, with the saints, now and then there are sinners
That live in the woods; and some half-breeds are wicked,
And know nothing of law unless taught by a bullet.
I've done what I could to teach knaves the commandments.
[Pg 88] Yes. Jack Whitcomb was brave. Brave as the bravest.
His glance was as keen and his mouth was as silent
As a trailer's should be who looks and who listens
By day and by night, having no one to talk to.
His finger was quick when it handled the trigger,
And his eye loved the sights as lightning loves rivers.
I've seen him stand up when the odds were against him.
Stand up like a man who takes coolly the chances.
That proves he was brave as I understand it.

One day we were boating on far Mistassinni.
We were fetching the portage above the great rapids,
Where they whirled, roaring down, freshet full, at their whitest,
[Pg 89] When we saw from a rock that stretched outward and over
The wild hissing water as it swept on in thunder,
A canoe coming down, rolling over and over,
With a little papoose clinging tight to the lashings;
And as it lanced by Jack went in like an otter.
How he did it God knows, but at the foot of the rapids,
Half a mile farther down racing onward, I found him
High and dry on the beach in a faint like a woman,
With the little papoose pulling away at his jacket.
And when he came to, he put child to his shoulder,
Nor stopped till it lay in the arms of its mother.

We were trailing, Henry and I, trailing and trapping
In the land to the north, where fur was the thickest,

[Pg 90] And knaves were as plenty as mink or as otter.
We took turns at sleeping, and trailed our line double
To keep our own skins, if we didn't get others.
It was folly to stay where we were, and we knew it,
For the knaves they got thicker, and soon there was shooting
Going on pretty lively. But we held to the business
And scouted the line once a week like true trappers.
And no accident happened save some holes in our jackets,
And my powder-horn emptied by a vagabond's bullet.
So we mended our clothing and felt pretty lively.
But the signs pointed one way. Our enemies thickened
Around us each day, and we weren't quite decided
[Pg 91] To stand in for a fight and settle the matter,
Or pull up our traps and get out of the country,
When it settled itself. And in this way it happened.

We were scouting the lake on the west shore one morning,
To find the knaves' camp and how many were in it,
When a short space ahead there came of a sudden
A crash as of thunder, and we knew that a dozen
Or twenty placed rifles had burst an ambushment.
And then in an instant there sounded another.
Two sharp, twin reports and the death yells that followed
Told us as we listened where the lead had been driven.
[Pg 92] Knew who he was? Of course. The man was Jack Whitcomb.
Do you think men who live by trapping and shooting
Don't learn to distinguish the voice of their rifles?
Jack was trailing the lake to find our encampment,
For far away in the south there had come to his cabin
A rumor that we in the north land were holding
Our line and our furs with a good deal of shooting.
So he left his own traps and came by swift trailing
To give us the help of another good rifle.
That was just like Jack Whitcomb. If you were in trouble
He was there by your side. You could always count on him,
With finger on trigger and both barrels loaded.
[Pg 93]
So Henry and I both took to our covers
Right and left of the trail Jack must take in retreating.

We didn't wait long, for the boy knew his business,
And soon he came backward, loading and running,
Like a man who was busy but wouldn't be hurried
Beyond his own gait, if he stopped there forever.
As he passed our two covers I piped him a whistle;
And he stopped in his tracks, and with low, pleasant laughter,
Stood there in full view coolly capping the nipples.
I have shot on each Gulf, both Southern and Northern.
I have trailed the long trail between either ocean.
Brave men I have seen, both in good and in evil,
But never a braver than the man called Jack Whitcomb.
[Pg 94] Well, why describe it? Call it scrimmage or battle,
It was done in a minute, or it may be a dozen.
It came like a whirlwind, and we three were in it
As men are in whirlwinds. It came like the thunder,
With a crash and a roar and a long running rumble
Dying down into silence. There were dead and some wounded,
And a few lucky knaves that fled wildly backward;
And Henry and I, when it passed, were left standing
By the body of him whose name was Jack Whitcomb,
Who lay as he fell, when headlong he tumbled,
His rifle still clinched and both barrels smoking.
[Pg 95] I have seen in my life many wounds made by bullets,
And a good many gashes by spear-points and arrows.
I have learned in my trailing a good many simples
Which have power to keep men from crossing the river
Before the Lord calls with voice that is certain.
And the wound that we found on Jack Whitcomb's body,
Though ugly and deep, was not beyond curing.

We cleansed and we stanched it and fought a brave battle
With death, for his life, and we won. For Jack mended.
We made a canoe and we bore him far southward.
A hundred good miles down the river we boated,
Till we came to his house of huge logs, strongly builded,
[Pg 96] Beneath the big pines on the bank of a rapid,
Which under it flowed its soft rush of brown water.
'Twas a place to bring peace to a heart that was troubled,
If peace might be found this side of the silence

Which brings peace to all that know sorrow in living.

Yes, we boated him down to his home by the rapids.
His home? No, rather his house let us call it.
For how can a house be a home with naught in it?
In house that is home must be love, warm and human,
A voice that is sweet, a heart that is gentle,
A soul that is true, and beside these a cradle
That prattles and coos; and the quick-falling patter
Of little white feet that run hither and thither.
[Pg 97] To his house, and not to his home, then, we brought him,
For certainly nothing and no one was in it,
Save himself and a dog, a bed and a table,
Some chairs, a few books, and a — Picture.
And this was the story that he told us in dying.
The man might have lived, beyond doubt, had he cared to.
But he didn't. No motive, he said. And he had none,
As we felt later on, when he told us his story.
So he died without word or sign. And in silence
We stood and saw him go forth on his journey
Without speaking a word, without a hand lifted
To hold or to stop him, for we did not feel certain
What was wisdom for one who went forth in such fashion.
Perhaps it was best he should go and be over
With pain, loss and trouble for ever and ever.
Henry says, it were well we should all of us go
[Pg 98] When life has no aim and no hope; and no doing
Remains to be done; and days are but eating
And drinking and breathing, only these and no more.

But before he went forth he gave me a message.
"I loved her," so his story began. Henry,
You remember the look on his face as he said it,
As he lay with his eyes fixed fast on the Picture?
"She was strong, and she drew me as life draws the young
And as death draws the old. I could not resist her.
She was vital with force, to attract and to hold.
She raced me a race for my life, and she won it.
I was man, not a boy, and I loved as man loves

When the forces of life are in him full-flooded
As rivers in meadows, when they flow to the sedges.
[Pg 99] Did she love me? Perhaps. Who can tell? She was woman,
And hence she was dark as the night, and as hidden!
Who could find her? Who the depth of her nature
Might measure? I tried but could not. Then boldly
I spake—spake as man speaks but once unto woman.
True and straight did I say it man fashion.
But she drew back offended; she shrank from my praying,
And with coldness of tone and suspicion dismissed me.
Had a man shown a tithe of that look in his eye,
On his face, he or I would have died on the instant.
But what can a man do, when scorned by a woman?
So I left her.
[Pg 100]
I need not say more. My life it was ended.
It wasn't worth living;—I am made in that fashion.
So I came to the woods. Where else when in trouble
Can man go and find what he needs, consolation?
·Go you down to her house, in the city, John Norton,
To the house where she lives, and give her this message.
Word for word let her hear it,—say where you left me.
There's gold in that box to pay your expenses.
Word for word as I tell you, nor say a word further."
Then he bade us good-by, and marched away bravely,
As a man on a trail that is somewhat uncertain.
And under the pines on the bank of the rapids
[Pg 101] We buried the man whom the woods called—Jack Whit-
comb,
And the picture he loved we placed on his bosom.

.   .   .   .

I went down to her house in the city. A cabin
Of stone, brown as tamarack bark, trimmed with olive.
It was high as a pine that stands on a mountain.
The door was as wide as the mouth of a cavern.
At the door stood a man rigged up like a soldier;

His face was as solemn as judgment to sinners;
He looked at me some, and I looked him all over,
Then he suddenly bowed like a half-breed with manners,
And told me to enter, and he would call Madame.
[Pg 102] The room was as large as a town house where settlers
Hold meetings to vote themselves office and wages.
The walls were like caves in far Arizona.
All covered with pictures of houses and battles;
Of ships blown onward by gales in mid-ocean;
Of children with wings, pretty queer-looking creatures;
Of men and of women, and some were half-naked.
But the floor was of oak, which gleamed like a polish;
And with mats thick as moss, and with skins it was covered,
So I felt quite at home, as there I stood looking,
And noting the size and signs of the cabin.

Then, all of a sudden, there came a soft rustle,
Like the rustle of leaves when the wind blows in autumn.
[Pg 103] And down the wide stairway across the great hall,
To the door of the room in which I was standing,
Stately and swift, came a woman and entered.
Tall as the tallest. Made firmly, knit firmly
Both in form and in limb, but full and well rounded;
Dark of eye, dark of face, with hair like a raven,
Like the girls of Nevada, where live the old races,
Whose blood is as fire, and whose skin is of olive,
Whose mouths are as sweet as a fig when it ripens.
Arms bare to the shoulders. Neck and bosom uncovered.
Her gown of white satin gleamed and flowed downward
And round her in folds of soft, creamy whiteness.
No ring on her hand, nor in ear. Not a circle
Of gold round her throat. One armlet of silver,
[Pg 104] And one at her wrist loosely clasped, small and slender.
So she entered and stood, and looked me all over.

Then slowly she spake. "Your name, sir, and business?"
"Madame," I said, "in the woods men call me John Norton;
John Norton, the Trapper." Then I stopped mighty sudden,
For her face it grew white to the lips and the chin,

And she swayed as a tree to the stroke of the chopper
When he sinks his axe in to the heart and it totters
And quivers. So I stopped, stopped quick and stood looking.

Then her dark face it lighted, and she said, speaking quickly:
[Pg 105] "John Norton, I know you. I know you are honest.
You live in the woods. You are good. I can trust you.
All men, I have heard, come to you in their trouble.
Have you seen in the North, have you met in the woods,
Has there come to your cabin a man, tall as you,
Brave as you and as tender? A man like to this?"
And out of her gown, from the folds on her bosom,
She lifted a locket of pearl-colored velvet,
Touched a spring, and I saw, as the lid of it opened,
The face of the man I and Henry had buried!

"John Norton," she cried, and her eyes burned like fever.
Her hand shook and trembled, her face was as marble,
[Pg 106] "Have you seen in the woods man like to this picture?
Speak quick and speak true as to woman in trouble.
For I did him great wrong, I thought he held lightly
My fair name and fame; held lightly my honor.
I thought he meant evil, and my heart, filled with anger,
Dismissed him in scorn; but I learned, I learned later,
He was true, and spake truth and loved me as heaven."

Then I stood and I looked and held my face steady,
So it gave her no sign of what I was thinking.
I saw she was honest, and I wished then to spare her,
But my word it was pledged, pledged to him in dying,
[Pg 107] To stand as I stood, face to face with this woman,
In her house, in that room, and give her his message.
Beside, not to know is far worse than the knowing
At times. So I rallied and told her the message,
Word for word, as he charged, the night he lay dying
In his house on the bank above the swift rapids.

"Madame," I said, "I have seen man like that picture,
Face and form. He was brave as you say. He was tender.

58

He was true unto death, and he loved you as heaven.
And these are the words that he sent you in dying.
I, a man of the woods, bring you this as last message,
[Pg 108] From one who now sleeps on the bank of the rapids
Of that northern river which pours its brown water
To the Lake of St. John from far Mistassinni.
'Tell her, John Norton, I loved her. Loved her in living,
With a love that was true, and with same love in dying.
Loved her like a man, like a saint, like a sinner,
For time now and time ever. That the one picture
She gave me I kept;—living, dying, and after.
That it lies on the breast of the man that you buried;
On the breast of the man who living did love her,
And that there it will lie until it shall crumble,
With heart underneath it, to dust. So tell her.
And in proof that I tell her the truth, and did tell it
[Pg 109] The night when we met, and I told her I loved her,
Give her this, the watch that I wore on the evening
We met, and the evening we parted. Let her open
And see. With her eyes let her see that I loved her.
So say and no more."

Thus I spake. Word for word as he told me I spake.
I gave her the watch, and I said no word further.
I had done as I pledged, I had said as he charged me,
So I stopped and stood waiting for word of dismissal.
But she said not a word, nor made she a sign.
The watch she took from me, touched the spring and it opened,
[Pg 110] And there, 'twixt the glass and the gold, withered and fad-
ed,
Lay a leaf of Red Rose. One leaf, and—no more.

For a moment she stood; stood, and gazed at the leaf,
Her face grew as white as her gown, and she trembled
And shook like a white swan in dying, then she cried,
"My God, I have killed him, my lover!"
And down on the floor, on the skins at her feet
She dropped as one stricken by bullet or lightning.

It was only last month that we two, in trailing,
Trailed a hundred good miles across to the rapids.
For we wanted to see before going northward
If evil had come to the grave of our comrade.
[Pg 111] But the grave lay untouched, by beast or by human.
The grass on the mound was well rooted and growthful.
At the foot of the grave the rose-tree I planted
Was as high as my head. And the leaves of the roses
Lay as thick as red snow-flakes on the mound that was under.
And we knew that on breast, as he slept, was her picture.
So we felt, as we gazed, it was well with Jack Whitcomb.

But often at night, when alone in my cabin,
I hear the low murmur of far northern rapids.
And often I see the great house and its splendor,
And wonder if death has helped the proud woman
To lay off her grief and escape from her sorrow.
[Pg 112] And blazed a line through the dark Valley of Shadow,
And brought her in peace to the edge of the clearing,
Where I know she would see Jack Whitcomb stand, waiting.

So I say it again, and I say it with knowledge,
That the woods have their sorrows as well as the cities.
And he knows but little of this great northern forest
Who thinks there's naught in it save trees, lakes, and mountains.

SELECT LIST

OF

Standard and Popular

BOOKS

PUBLISHED BY

<u>DEWOLFE, FISKE & CO.,</u>

361-365 WASHINGTON STREET, BOSTON, MASS.

Any Book On This List Will Be Sent, Postpaid, On Receipt Of Price.

*IN ADDITION to the works mentioned
in this list, we will furnish any books
in the market at lowest possible prices, and
would respectfully solicit correspondence in
regard to prices or any desired information.*

DEWOLFE, FISKE & CO., Boston, Mass.

*P.S.--Catalogue of books at special reductions
mailed free to any address.*

Boston, Mass.

Standard and Popular Books

PUBLISHED BY

DeWolfe, Fiske & Co.,

PUBLISHERS, GENERAL BOOKSELLERS, AND
LIBRARY AGENTS,

Boston, Mass.

******* *In order to insure the correct delivery of the actual works, or particular Editions specified in this List, the name of the Publishers should be distinctly given. These books can be had from any local bookseller; but should any difficulty be experienced in procuring them, Messrs. DeWolfe, Fiske & Co., will be happy to forward them direct, postage paid, on receipt of cheque, stamps or Postal order for the amount, with a copy of their complete catalogue.*

New Editions of W. H. H. Murray's Famous Books.

DAYLIGHT LAND. The experiences, incidents, and adventures, humorous and otherwise, which befell Judge John Doe, Tourist, of San Francisco; Mr. Cephas Pepperell, Capitalist, of Boston; Colonel Goffe, the man from New Hampshire, and divers others, in their Parlor-Car Excursion over Prairie and Mountain; as recorded and set forth by W. H. H. Murray. Superbly illustrated with 150 cuts in various colors by the best artists. 8vo, 350 pages. Unique paper covers, $2.50; cloth, $3.50; cloth, extra gilt, $4.00.

The New York Herald; says,

Impossible to find a handsomer book on outdoor life than this. The author's peculiar faculty for describing days in the woods and rambles with good company has long been known. "Daylight Land" is longer than the book in which the same author made the Adirondacks seem some other place to men whose eyes were not as wide-open as his own, and the style is even breezier, if that is possible. Seldom does a book appear which is so entirely creditable to author, artist, and publisher.

HOW DEACON TUBMAN AND PARSON WHITNEY KEPT NEW YEAR'S, and Other Stories. By W. H. H. Murray, author of "Adirondack Tales," etc. 12mo. Illustrated. $1.25.

Deacon Tubman, a jolly, fat, good-natured man, is presented with a woollen night-cap on New Year's morning by his housekeeper, "a typical spinster not overburdened with fat." This so rejoices the

Deacon that he is possessed to make others happy, goes to call upon his pastor, and makes him leave his books and spend the day skating, sleighing, and driving with his parishioners.

STORY THE KEG TOLD ME, AND THE STORY OF THE MAN WHO DIDN'T KNOW MUCH. By W. H. H. Murray, author of "Daylight Land," "Adirondack Adventures," etc. 12mo. Cloth, $1.50.

"Two admirable stories by W. H. H. Murray, in both which appears John Norton, the trapper, a character that promises to become as much of a favorite as is the hero of the Leather Stocking novels. These stories have a bracing outdoor freshness and a delightfully crisp realism: are vigorous in tone, and strong and picturesque in the relation. Taken altogether, they may be pronounced in the most artistic of Mr. Murray's excursions into the realms of fiction, and fascinating generally." — *Saturday Evening Gazette.*

DEACONS. By W. H. H. Murray. 16mo. Paper, 50 cts. Cloth, 75 cts.

"Mr. Murray is an expert in the art of character drawing; he can manipulate humor and pathos with equal facility. No one will gainsay their freshness and individuality."—*N. Y. Commercial Advertiser.*

ADIRONDACK ADVENTURES. "In the Wilderness; or, Camp Life in the Adirondacks." By W. H. H. Murray, 12mo. Illustrated. Paper, 50 cts. Cloth, $1.25.

"In the 'Adventures in the Wilderness' W. H. H. Murray strikes the happy hunting ground, which long ago earned for him the popular title, 'Adirondack Murray,' and here, as in his other books, he fairly revels in stirring incident, lively and faithful conception of character, and the powerful but delightful description of natural scenery which have already given his work an enviable and lasting place in American literature."—*Nashville American.*

THE BUSTED EX-TEXAN, AND OTHER STORIES. By W. H. H. Murray. With photogravure portrait of Mr. Murray, and eight full-page il-

lustrations by Thos. Worth. Square 12mo. Cloth,
$1.00.

**CIVILIZATION IN THE UNITED STATES,
AND OTHER ESSAYS CONCERNING AMERI-
CA.** By Matthew Arnold. 16mo. Unique paper
boards, 50 cts. Cloth, uncut, $1.25. The cloth bind-
ing matches the uniform edition of his collected
works. Comprises the critical essays, which created
so much discussion, namely, "General Grant, an
Estimate," "A Word About America," "A Word
More About America," and "Civilization in the
United States." The collection gathers in the great
critic's last contribution to literature.

Bulfinch's Mythology.

**THE AGE OF CHIVALRY; Or Legends of King
Arthur.** "Stories of the Round Table," "The Cru-
sades," "Robin Hood," etc. By Thomas Bulfinch. A
new and enlarged edition. Revised by Rev. E. E.
Hale. Large 12mo. Illustrated. $2.50.

In "The Age of Fable," Mr. Bulfinch endeavored to impart the
pleasure of classical learning to the English reader by presenting the
stories of Pagan mythology in a form adapted to modern taste. In
this volume the attempt has been made to treat in the same way the
stories of the second "age of fable"—the age which witnessed the
dawn of the several states of modern Europe.

**THE AGE OF FABLE; Or, Beauties of Mythol-
ogy.** By Thomas Bulfinch. A new and enlarged edition, containing over 100 illustrations from ancient
paintings and statuary. Revised by Rev. E. E. Hale.
Large 12mo. $2.50.

Young readers will find this book a source of entertainment; those
more advanced, a useful companion in their reading; those who
travel and visit museums and galleries of art, an interpreter of
paintings and sculptures.

LEGENDS OF CHARLEMAGNE; Or, Romance of the Middle Ages. Stories of Paladin and Saracen. By Thomas Bulfinch. 12mo. Illustrated. $2.50.

Prof. Clark Murray's Works.

SOLOMON MAIMON: An Autobiography. Translated from the German, with Additions and Notes, by Prof. J. Clark Murray. Cr. 8vo. Cloth. 307 pages. $2.00.

The London *Spectator* says: "Dr. Clark Murray has had the rare good fortune of first presenting this singularly vivid book in an English translation as pure and lively as if it were an original, and an original by a classic English writer."

George Eliot, in "Daniel Deronda," mentions it as "that wonderful bit of autobiography—the life of the Polish Jew, Solomon Maimon:" and Milman, in his "History of the Jews," refers to it as a curious and rare book.

HANDBOOK OF PSYCHOLOGY. By Prof. J. Clark Murray, LL.D., Professor of Mental and Moral Philosophy, M'Gill College, Montreal. Cr. 8vo. 2d edition, enlarged and improved. $1.75.

Clearly and simply written, with illustrations so well chosen that the dullest student can scarcely fail to take an interest in the subject.

Adopted for use in colleges in Scotland, England, Canada, and the United States.

Prof. Murray's good fortune in bringing to light the "Maimon Memoirs," together with the increasing popularity of his "Handbook of Psychology," has attracted the attention of the intellectual world, giving him a position with the leaders of thought of the present age. His writings are at once original and suggestive.

The Popular Works of Sally Pratt McLean.

CAPE COD FOLKS. A Novel. Twenty-third edition. Illustrated. 12mo. Cloth, $1.25. Paper, 50 cents.

TOWHEAD: THE STORY OF A GIRL. Fifth Thousand. 12mo. Cloth, $1.25. Paper, 50 cents.

Since the production of Miss McLean's first effort "Cape Cod Folks," she has steadily advanced in intellectual development; the same genius is at work in a larger and more artistic manner, until she has at length produced what must be truly considered as her masterpiece, and which we have the pleasure to announce for immediate publication.

SOME OTHER FOLKS. A Book in Four Stories. 12mo. Cloth, $1.25. Paper, 50 cents.

These books are so well known that further comment seems superfluous. Suffice it to say that the entire press of the country has unanimously spoken of them in terms of high praise, dwelling not only on their delicious humor, their literary workmanship, their genuine pathos, and their real power and eloquence, but what has been described as their deep, true *humanness*, and the inimitable manner in which the mirror is held up to nature that all may see reflected therein some familiar trait, some description or character which is at once recognized.

LASTCHANCE JUNCTION: HUMAN NATURE IN THE FAR WEST. A Novel. By Sally Pratt McLean. 1 vol. 12mo. Cloth, $1.25.

"Terse, incisive descriptions of men and scenery, drawn with so vivid a pen that one can see the characters and their setting, delicious bits of humor, passages full of infinite pathos, make this book absolutely hold the reader from the title to the last word, and as, when finished, one sighs for the pity of it, the feeling rises that such a work has not been written in vain, and will have its place among those which tend to elevate our race."

MISS FRANCES MERLEY. A Novel. By John Elliot Curran. 420 pages. Square 16mo. Paper covers, 50 cents. Cloth, $1.00.

The first important work of an author familiar to American readers by his remarkable sketches to *Scribner's* and other magazines.

AUTOBIOGRAPHY OF A NEW ENGLAND FARM HOUSE: A Romance of the Cape Cod Lands. By N. H. Chamberlain. 380 pages. Square 16mo. Paper covers, 50 cents. Cloth, $1.00.

A novel of singular power and beauty, great originality and rugged force. Born and bred on Cape Cod, the author, at the winter firesides of country people, very conservative of ancient English customs now gone, heard curious talk of kings, Puritan ministers, the war and precedent struggle of our Revolution, and touched a race of men and women now passed away. He also heard, chiefly from ancient women, the traditions of ghosts, witches and Indians, as they are preserved, and to a degree believed, by honest Christian folk, in the very teeth of modern progress.

<table>
<tr><td></td><td>*Publishers,*</td><td></td></tr>
<tr><td>*DeWolfe, Fiske & Co.*</td><td>*Booksellers,*</td><td>*BOSTON.*</td></tr>
<tr><td></td><td>*Library Agents.*</td><td></td></tr>
</table>